# Uncle Frank's PIT

# For Moose, Pidge, and, of course, Christy

VIKING
Published by the Penguin Group
Penguin Putnam Inc., 375 Hudson Street, New York, New York 10014, U.S.A.
Penguin Books Ltd, 27 Wrights Lane, London W8 5TZ, England
Penguin Books Australia Ltd, Ringwood, Victoria, Australia
Penguin Books Canada Ltd, 10 Alcorn Avenue, Toronto, Ontario, Canada M4V 3B2
Penguin Books (N.Z.) Ltd, 182-190 Wairau Road, Auckland 10, New Zealand

Penguin Books Ltd, Registered Offices: Harmondsworth, Middlesex, England

First published in 1998 by Viking, a member of Penguin Putnam Books for Young Readers

1 3 5 7 9 10 8 6 4 2

LIBRARY OF CONGRESS CATALOGING-IN-PUBLICATION DATA
McElligott, Matthew.
Uncle Frank's pit / Matthew McElligott.
p. cm.
Summary: Eccentric Uncle Frank comes for a short visit, but ends
up moving into a pit in the backyard while he tries to dig up
something he thinks is buried there.
ISBN: 0-670-87737-9
[1. Uncles—Fiction. 2. Humorous stories.] I. Title.
PZ7.M478448Un 1998 [E]—dc21 97-27303 CIP AC

Printed in Hong Kong
Set in Berliner Grotesk

# Uncle Frank's PIT

## by Matthew McElligott

**VIKING**

Last summer we invited Uncle Frank to visit us.

Surprisingly, he did.

You see, Uncle Frank never visited *anyone*. In fact, he seldom left his workshop.

He even slept there.

Just the same, we always invited him.

"I can only stay a few hours," said Uncle Frank. "I'm in the middle of an important project."

A month later, he was still with us.
"So, Frank," said my dad, "how about
that important project?"
"Project?" said Uncle Frank.
"Oh, that can wait. What's for dinner?"

One morning I woke up to a strange sound coming from the backyard. Uncle Frank was hopping in circles holding a long stick in front of him. Hanging from the end of the stick was a rusty coat hanger. The antenna from our old TV was taped to his hat. "Hmm . . ." said Uncle Frank every few minutes.

That night at dinner, Uncle Frank said, "I have something very important to tell you all."

"You're leaving?" said my dad. "Already?"

"Heavens no," said Uncle Frank. "In fact, it looks like I'll be here quite a while. I've done some tests, and I've discovered something very interesting."

My dad began to fidget in his chair.

"Did you know," said Uncle Frank, "there are dinosaur bones buried in your backyard?"

"You can't be serious," said my mom.

"Impossible," said my dad.

"Then it's settled," said Uncle Frank. "I'll start digging tomorrow."

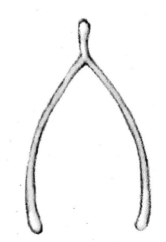

For the next week I helped Uncle Frank dig. Before long the hole was pretty deep.

"You know what I hate?" said Uncle Frank one afternoon. "I hate climbing out of this hole every time we want to take a break."

I thought about it for a minute. "We've got some old furniture in the basement."

"Super," said Uncle Frank.

We spent the afternoon lowering some old chairs and a table down into the pit. Uncle Frank arranged them in a circle.

"All the comforts of home!" said Uncle Frank.

As the days went by, Uncle Frank started moving more and more things into the hole.

First he brought down a radio so he could listen to music while he worked. Then he added lanterns for digging after dark. He set up a cot so he could spend the night, and he even hung pictures on the wall.

After two weeks of digging we hadn't found a single dinosaur bone.

"What's the rush?" said Uncle Frank.

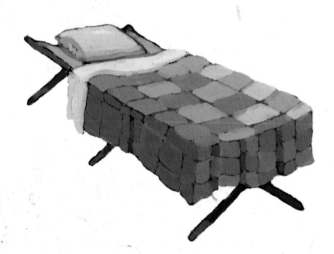

"Frank," said my dad one morning, "I've been doing some reading. If there really are any bones down there . . ."

"Not bones," said Uncle Frank. "I did more tests. It's oil."

"Oil?" said my dad.

"In fact," said Uncle Frank, "we're so close I can almost smell it."

"It smells?" said my dad.

"By the way," said Uncle Frank, "can I borrow the TV and a really long extension cord?"

The next weekend, Uncle Frank said to my mom, "Is it okay if I have a few friends over tonight?"

"Of course!" said my mom. "Just give me a few minutes to tidy up the house."

"That won't be necessary," said Uncle Frank.

That night I got up around midnight to get a glass of water. Uncle Frank's party was still going strong.

A few weeks later, the plumber showed up. He said he had Uncle Frank's hot tub. My dad flipped his lid.

"This has gone far enough!" he shouted. "It's time we told Frank a thing or two."

"Go easy on him, honey," said my mom. "He means well."

Uncle Frank was in the backyard putting in a mailbox.

"Frank," said my dad, "we need to talk."

"Talk?" said Uncle Frank. "Sure! Come on down. I've got snacks."

One by one we climbed down
into the hole. Uncle Frank turned on the lights.
"I don't believe it," said my dad.
"Oh my," said my mom.
"Cool!" I said.

"Hey, Frank!" said the plumber. "Where do you want this thing?"

"Over in the corner," said Uncle Frank.

"Frank, enough is enough," said my dad. "You can't live here. This isn't your house. It's a hole in the ground."

"He's right," said my mom. "You *have* been down here almost two months. Maybe you were mistaken about the bones."

"Oil," said my dad.

"Treasure!" said Uncle Frank. "And there's no mistake. These things just take time. I'll be done by Christmas."

"Christmas!" said my dad. "Christmas!" He started to hop up and down.

"Hey, Frank," said the plumber. "What's this?"

"What's what?" said Uncle Frank.

"This thing buried in the corner. It's blocking my pipes."

"It's probably just a rock," said Uncle Frank. "Dig around it."

"It doesn't look like a rock," said my dad. "Hand me the shovel."

"How about a pretzel instead?" said Uncle Frank.

"Later," said my dad. Everyone gathered around as he began to dig.

"Keep at it," said my mom. "I think there's something there."

I could see it too. It was definitely not a rock.

"Frank," said my dad, "I think you've done it!"

Uncle Frank was speechless.

For a few weeks, things were pretty crazy.
The newspapers came and took our pictures,
and we even got to be on TV.

We gave the statue to the museum.
They put up a plaque with Uncle Frank's name on it.
He didn't seem to care.

One morning when we came down for breakfast Uncle Frank was waiting for us at the table. He had his suitcase with him, and he was wearing his hat. The rest of his body was covered in aluminum pie plates. He looked happier than he had in weeks.

"Frank," said my dad, "you're not leaving, are you?"

"I'm afraid so," said Uncle Frank. As he stood, the pie plates made a sound like wind chimes. "I've had a lovely visit. But . . . I'm picking up some signals."

"What kind of signals?" said my mom.

"I'm not sure," said Uncle Frank, "but it's something big. Over near Aunt Edith's place. I'd better check it out."

"Frank," said my dad, "come back and visit us anytime."

**"You can count on it," said Uncle Frank.**